Second Leaves
Growing Young Gardeners

by Mary A. Agria

Author of the best-selling *TIME in a Garden*

with illustrations by photographer John J. Agria

Profound thanks to Joyce Giguere and Ellen McGill for their generous support
and patient editing as well as conceptual advice. You're the best!
Deepest appreciation to: master gardeners David Kidd and Jean Long
for their technical assistance, encouragement and shared love of all things 'garden';
educational consultant Janet Beam Smith for her expertise and technical editing;
Jenna Clarkson and Adriane Agria for volunteering time in their garden;
and Laurie Zmrzlik for the cover shot of author Agria's garden.
Above all, I express my heartfelt thanks to my husband and agent, John,
for his amazing photography and unfailing support. You've made this a true labor of love.

To learn more about the author's LIFE IN THE GARDEN series,
read sample chapters of her novels or arrange for talks or signings,
go to http://www.maryagria.com

I like to walk in the garden with Grandma.

She always listens. I talk and talk.

Grandma shows me all the plants.

She tells me how the plants grow.

"Most plants need seeds to grow," Grandma says.
She shows me how to plant a seed in the ground.
The seeds are very small. I learn to plant them.
I dig a hole in the ground and put the seeds in it.
Then I cover the tiny seeds with soil.

GRANDMA SAYS: Some seeds need deep holes. Others should not be very deep. Seeds for vegetables often need straight rows. We can use a stake to mark where seeds are planted.

I learn to take care of the seeds.

The seeds are very thirsty. I give them water.

Seeds need food to help them grow.

The food is called *fertilizer* or *compost*.

GRANDMA SAYS: Compost is made from dead leaves, vegetable scraps or other plant material. We mix, shred and dig the compost into the ground around the plants.

The sun shone. The rain came. Then one morning we saw something new in the garden. A tiny green thing stuck its head out of the ground. Grandma said, "It is a baby plant. We call it a *shoot*."

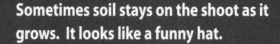
Sometimes soil stays on the shoot as it grows. It looks like a funny hat.

The shoots grew and grew. They stood together like trees in a tiny woods. We had to give them more space to grow. Grandma called it **thinning**.

"They are not babies any more," Grandma said. "They are seedlings. They are young plants now." "Like me," I said.

Grandma smiled.

GRANDMA SAYS: The seedling stems are tiny. We have to be careful not to break them.

The tiny seedlings grew taller and taller.
One day, Grandma and I had a surprise.
In the middle of the seed leaves,
we saw a funny bump.
The tiny bump grew and grew.
"That looks like a new
leaf," I said.

How many "bumps" do you see?

These new leaves did not look like the first ones.

"They are **second** or *true* leaves," Grandma said.

"They show us how a plant looks when it is big."

Some true or second leaves had fur.

Some were fat.

Some were long and thin.

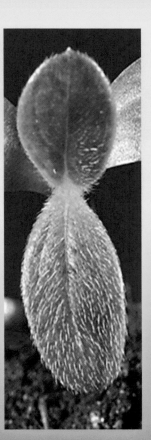

Some were round.

Some had sharp points.

Some looked like stars or feathers.

Coneflower Cosmos Daisy Lupine

Now when Grandma looked at the leaves,
she could tell the names of all the plants.

"Are the plants grown up yet?" I said.

Grandma said, "Not yet, but soon."

"Like me," I said. Grandma smiled.

Hollyhock Phlox Poppy Sunflower

Coneflower   Cosmos   Daisy   Lupine

When we walked in the garden,

plants had flowers now. They all looked different.

I tried to learn their names.

"But sometimes I forget," I said.

"Sometimes I forget, too," Grandma said.

Grandma and I laughed.

Can you find bees on this page? They help make the garden grow, too.

Hollyhock   Phlox   Poppy   Sunflower

"A garden is like a big family," Grandma said. The plants all live and grow together. Some are big. Some are small. But all of them are special. All of them have a story.

Grandma and I are making our own Garden Book about all my favorite plants.

Coneflower

Cosmos

Daisy

Hollyhock

Lupine

Phlox

Poppy

Sunflower

The seeds are shown at their actual size. Can you find 2 busy bees that live in my garden?

GRANDMA SAYS: All of these plants love sun, but others grow better in the shade. We need to put plants where they are happy. Some like water, some do not. Size is not important. The poppy has tiny seeds, but its leaves are big. Phlox seeds are small, but the plant can be short or tall. A garden looks best with plants in many sizes, shapes and colors.

Coneflower

The petals of this flower grow in a circle.
Sharp spines grow in the middle.
They look like a prickly ice cream cone.
Butterflies love the bright pink color.
Coneflowers love the sun.

First or Seed Leaves   Second or True Leaves   Adult Leaves

Seed leaves are fat, rounded. True ones grow thin and pointed. Older ones have wrinkles.

GRANDMA SAYS: Coneflower is also called *Echinacea.* That word means "hedgehog", which is a prickly animal. Why do you think it has that name? The flowers bloom in late summer. Some coneflower plants are used to make medicine. Coneflowers do not need much water.

Cosmos

Flowers that look like this are
really TWO different flowers in ONE.
There is a round ring of petals.
In the middle there is a circle
made up of tiny flowers [called florets].
Bees and butterflies love cosmos.

First [seed] Leaves	Second [true] Leaves	Adult Cosmos Leaves

First leaves are skinny. Second and adult leaves look soft and feathery.

GRANDMA SAYS: I have the whole world in my garden. Cosmos first came from Mexico and the deserts in the western U.S. People named this flower "cosmos" because it looks like the sun with all the planets in a circle or rings around it.

Daisy

Daisies belong to the sunflower family. The yellow center and the circle of petals look like a sun with rays shining around it.
It is fun to make daisy chains from flowers and stems.

First [seed] Leaves	Second [true] Leaves	Adult Daisy Leaves

First leaves are fat and round. Second or adult leaves look like canoe paddles.

GRANDMA SAYS: Daisy is from an Old Saxon word that means "days eye". A daisy is really TWO flowers. It has petals and center florets. We play a game pulling off one petal after another. We say, " love-me-love-me-not". But my Grandma says that she loves ME all the time.

Hollyhocks

These plants can grow very tall.
The flowers and leaves are also very big.
Many big flowers grow up and down
on the tall stems.

Flowers can be many colors, from white
to dark red, yellow and even purple.

Seed Leaves   **Second Leaves**   **Adult Leaves**

Seed leaves have veins like a hand. Second and adult ones have jagged edges.

GRANDMA SAYS: These plants come from far away, in Asia. The flowers look like dancers who are twirling in big, fluffy skirts. Pioneer children used the flowers as dolls. Hollyhock leaves curl in the hot sun.

Lupine

Lupine [loo-pin] flowers
grow like giant fireworks on tall stems.
This is a member of the pea family.
The lupine seeds grow
inside of hard shells or *pods*.

First [seed] Leaves   Second [true] Leaves   Adult Lupine Leaves

First leaves are round and shiny. Second and adult leaves look like big stars.

GRANDMA SAYS: Some lupines do not have flowers every single year [*biennials*] .
"Bi" means two.   One year biennial plants will blossom. One year they will rest.
Flowers that bloom or have flowers every year are called "perennials".

Phlox

Phlox sounds like 'flocks' and
they grow close together
in thick clumps. The flowers
can be pink, purple and even white.
Phlox plants can grow very tall
or be very short and creep along the ground.
Deer and rabbits love to eat them.

First [seed] Leaves	Second [true] Leaves	Adult Leaves

First leaves look fat and rounded. Second and adult leaves are long and narrow.

GRANDMA SAYS: The picture of the short purple flowers shows a dwarf or creeping phlox.
Phlox like the big white flowers in the picture can grow very tall. Some phlox smell very sweet.

Poppy

Poppy seeds are very tiny.
Grandma says it is easier
if we grow some poppies
from small pieces of grown-up
plants. Flowers are red, orange,
white or yellow. Poppy leaves have prickly spines,
but not all leaves and flowers look the same.
Some poppy seeds are used for baking cakes and cookies.

California poppy

Oriental poppy

California poppy

Oriental poppy

First [seed] Leaves   Second Leaves   Two different adult poppy leaves.

GRANDMA SAYS: Some poppy plants only live and grow for one year. We call them *annuals*.
Other poppy plants come back every single year. They are called *perennials*.

Sunflower

This plant only lives for a year.
It is called an annual.
Some sunflower plants grow
ten feet tall. Birds and people
love to eat the sunflower seeds.

Seed leaves turn
yellow and fall off.

Second Leaves

Adult Leaves

Seed Leaves

First leaves are shiny. Second are furry. Adult leaves are big and wrinkled.

GRANDMA SAYS: Baby sunflower plant leaves will move to follow the sun. This is called *heliotropism*. The flowers are made of petals and 1 to 2 thousand mini-flowers or florets. The seeds also grow in the center of the flower. Cooking oil is made from the seeds.

"Wow!" I said. "Plants come in so many shapes and sizes."
"So do gardens," Grandma said.

A garden can be as BIG as a park.
A garden can be as small as a pot.
"But do you know what?" I said.
"The very best garden in the whole wide world, is the one that WE can grow

...together!"

GRANDMA SAYS: We learn a lot when we look at other people's gardens.

Some gardens look wild. Some look very formal. Some just grow one plant.

Others grow many different plants. What kind of garden do *YOU* like best?

Allium Columbine Bleeding Heart Foxglove Iris Peony

Bulb **These plants bloom or have flowers in spring.** *Tuber* *Shoots/roots*

Astilbe Brown-Eyed Susan Bellflower Lily Mallow Monarda

Tubers OR Bulbs

These plants have flowers in summer.

Sedum Hellebore

Fall and Winter

What do YOU want to grow in YOUR garden?

GRANDMA SAYS: Not all plants grow from seeds. Some grow from bulbs or tubers. Tubers/bulbs do not have second leaves. They keep the same leaves when they grow up. But THAT is another story ! A good garden has plants that will bloom at every season. Spring, summer, fall and even winter, gardens are a year-'round adventure !

SECOND LEAVES: *PARENT-TEACHER GUIDE*

Adults who garden are in an unique position to encourage a child's growth from "seedlings" or sprouts into loved and self-confident teens and adults. Time in the garden together teaches a child to recognize and appreciate his or her uniqueness and individuality—our 'Second Leaves'—when they begin to appear. Even young children can discover not just the growth stages of plants, but gain precious insights into the miracle of "becoming".

Young gardeners learn hands-on what it means TO GROW.

When a plant first pops up or "sprouts" (called a seedling), it has 3 parts:
1) ROOTS [under the ground, anchoring a plant]
2) SHOOTS
3) SEED LEAVES

A FUN GAME: Together sing a plant version of "head-shoulders-knees-toes":
ROOTS n SHOOTS n SEED LEAVES, TOO. SEED LEAVES, TOO. PLANTS ARE GROWING.

Soon first or seed leaves [A] begin to dry up and disappear. By then the second or true leaves [B] have formed---a transition to adulthood for the plant. Adult plants become busy chemical factories, capable of photosynthesis. They use energy from the sun to change carbon dioxide into organic compounds, especially sugars. Photosynthesis in adult plants is important for sustaining all life on the planet.

- *Creating a Garden Book encourages children to be more observant about what they experience.*
- *The last text page invites readers to create their own Garden Plan, with some plants that DON'T grow from seeds (like bulbs and tubers). Use it also to illustrate the 2 main classes of flowering plants:*

1) MONOCOTS [monocotoledons] have only 1 blade-shaped leaf. They do not have second leaves. Famous monocots: daffodils, iris, lilies and tulips. Some 50 to 60 thousand species, including agricultural plants like grains, grasses, onions and garlic, fall into this category.
2) DICOTS [dicotoledons] have 2 fatter "seed" leaves and develop second leaves. Dicots include 300 + flowering plants (8 are featured in this book), some 195,000 species.

CPSIA information can be obtained
at www.ICGtesting.com
Printed in the USA
LVIC06n0008051017
551238LV00014B/72